Icarus Swinebuckle

Michael Garland

Albert Whitma... ...n Grove, Illinois

Library of Congress Cataloging-in-Publication Data

Garland, Michael, 1952-

Icarus Swinebuckle / written and illustrated by Michael Garland.

p. cm.

Summary: Although he knows that his ambition to fly is silly,

Icarus the pig sets out to design, build, and test a set of wings.

ISBN 0-8075-3495-1

[1. Pigs Fiction. 2. Flight Fiction] I. Title.

PZ7.G18413Ic 2000

[Fic]–dc21 99-16880

CIP

For my wife, Peggy

I CARUS SWINEBUCKLE worked as a cobbler, but he was really a dreamer. He should have spent his days hammering away in his shop, making and mending shoes, but instead he stared out the window at birds, butterflies, and bugs–anything that could fly.

Icarus's greatest wish was to fly. He knew it was a silly hope for a portly pig, but still, flying was all he could think about. Night and day he sketched inventions or made little models in the back room of his shop. If people asked what he was doing, Icarus would always explain–and everyone would laugh. Who ever heard of a flying pig?

The only person who believed in him was his little son, Robin. When Icarus said he could fly, Robin Swinebuckle knew it was true.

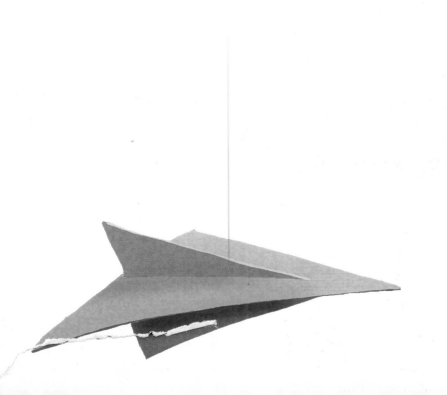

The shelves of the shop were piled high with shoes to be fixed. Customers were waiting for new shoes they had ordered, too.

"Oh, Icarus," his wife, Peggy, pleaded one day, "you must forget all this silly daydreaming. We need money to pay the rent!"

"I know, Peg. Yes, dear, I know," said Icarus with a sigh.

Lady Holstein and her sister marched into the shop. "Mr. Swinebuckle, I came to pick up my shoes. I hope they're ready this time!"

"Oh, Lady Holstein, I've been so busy with this and that…I promise your shoes will be next on my list."

"Really!" Lady Holstein bellowed. "From now on, I'll take my business elsewhere!"

With that, the two cows turned their backs and stormed out, their fine gowns fluttering behind them.

The door opened again. Icarus froze; it was his landlord, Mr. Gnawbone.
"I've come for the rent!" the wolf demanded in a voice like a rusty hinge.
"Hello, Mr. Gnawbone," replied Icarus nervously. "Uh…we're a little behind
around here, but we'll have your money by the end of the week."

"Late again!" growled the wolf. "You're not like your father. He was the greatest cobbler in all of East London. *He* was never late with his rent!"

Icarus could only look at the floor. He knew Mr. Gnawbone was right.

"Remember, Swinebuckle, we *all* have to eat," said the wolf with an evil smile.

Mr. Gnawbone went out, and Icarus began to tremble. If only he could concentrate on shoes instead of flying!

That night, after the shop was closed, Icarus took Robin into the back room. "Look at this," he said. "I think it might work."

There on the worktable was the most beautiful pair of wings Robin had ever seen.
"I made them from goose feathers and wax," explained Icarus.
"They look like an angel's wings," whispered Robin.

By now Icarus was the talk of the town. A pig who thought he could fly! What foolishness! On the day Icarus planned to test his wings, a noisy crowd gathered around his shop. When he finally squeezed out of his attic window and onto the roof, the mob had jammed the nearby streets and alleyways. Folks even stood on the dock that stretched into the river.

As Icarus tiptoed to the peak of the roof, a great roar rose from the mass of upturned faces. He raised his arms and spread his wings.

The crowd fell silent. Peggy Swinebuckle hid her eyes–she couldn't watch.
Robin stood proudly, waiting to see his father fly.

Holding his wings high, Icarus stepped into thin air. A gasp came up from the crowd. Icarus flapped his wings, wildly at first, but he didn't fall. He gained confidence, rising higher and higher. The crowd screamed and cheered.

Icarus Swinebuckle was earthbound no more!

Icarus rose far above the earth. He flew to a low cloud, then to higher and higher ones. Now he could see only the sun. Could he fly there? He had to try. Icarus began beating his wings with all his might.

As he drew closer to the blazing sun, the wax of Icarus's wings began to soften. One feather fell off, then another. His wings were melting! Icarus stopped climbing, but it was too late.

He began to drop, slowly at first. Then, suddenly, he plummeted back to earth.

Everyone was still staring at the sky. When they saw Icarus streaking back down like a comet with a tail of feathers, they tried to flee.

Too late! Icarus plunged into the river with an amazing bellyflop. *Splat!*
The awestruck onlookers were soaked with muddy water.

Icarus popped to the surface like a fuzzy pink cork.
When they fished him out, he was unhurt—except for his pride.
He could see now that he shouldn't have tried to fly to the sun.
Maybe he shouldn't have tried to fly at all!

But there was Robin, smiling proudly. Mrs. Swinebuckle gave her husband
a big kiss. And another cheer went up from the crowd!

Even Mr. Gnawbone looked impressed. "That's my tenant!" he was telling anyone who would listen. "Icarus Swinebuckle lives in my building! The pig who can fly is my tenant!"

That night in his workshop, Icarus told Robin all about the adventure.

"When I was above the clouds, the air was so clear I could see the moon. I had an idea for a flying ship that could take us there. I wonder if I could build it…"

"I'll help you, Father!" Robin said.

Icarus nodded. Then he picked up his sketch book and began to draw.